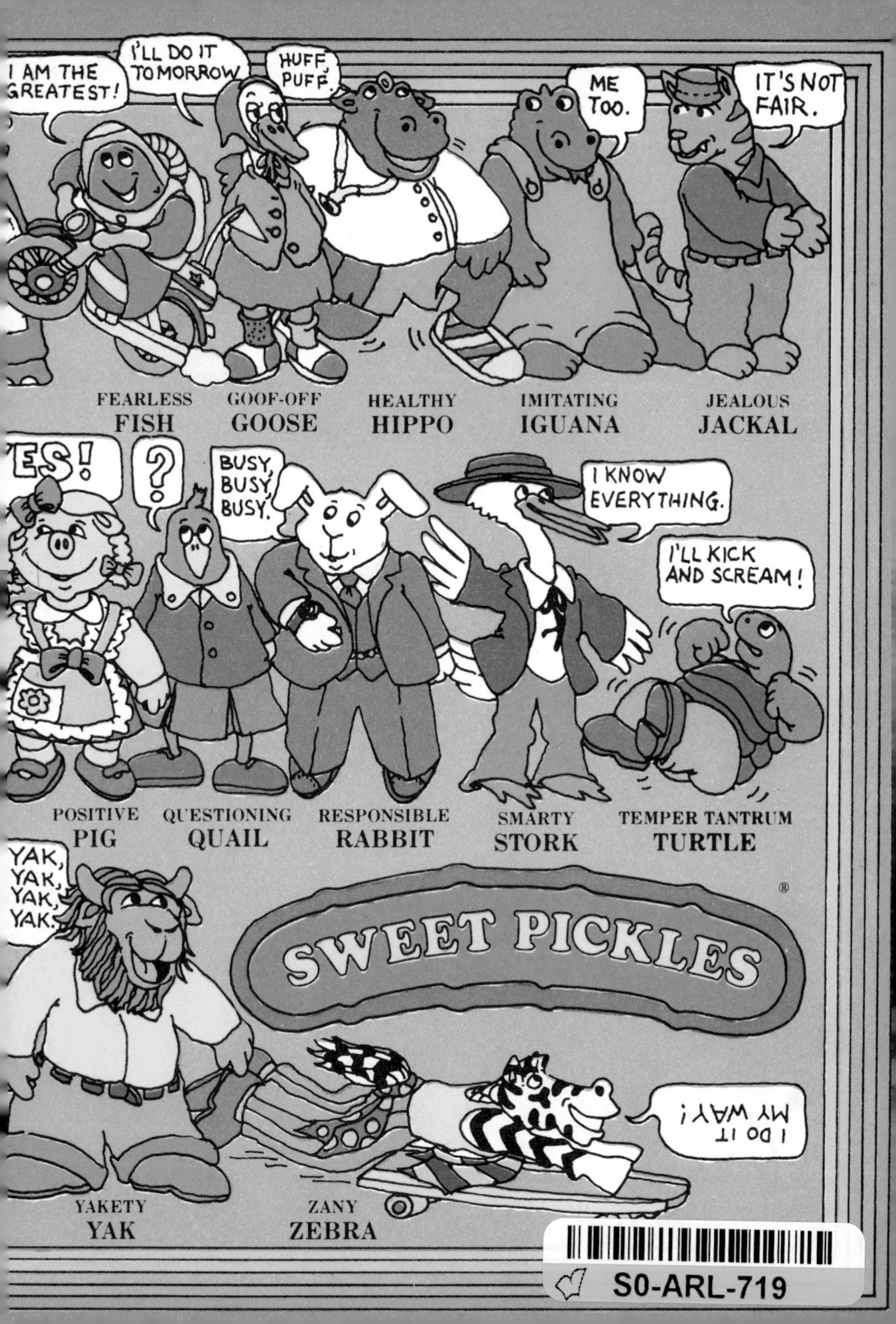
I AM THE GREATEST!
I'LL DO IT TOMORROW
HUFF, PUFF.
ME TOO.
IT'S NOT FAIR.
FEARLESS FISH
GOOF-OFF GOOSE
HEALTHY HIPPO
IMITATING IGUANA
JEALOUS JACKAL
ES!
?
BUSY, BUSY, BUSY.
I KNOW EVERYTHING.
I'LL KICK AND SCREAM!
POSITIVE PIG
QUESTIONING QUAIL
RESPONSIBLE RABBIT
SMARTY STORK
TEMPER TANTRUM TURTLE
YAK, YAK, YAK, YAK.
SWEET PICKLES®
I DO IT MY WAY!
YAKETY YAK
ZANY ZEBRA
S0-ARL-719

In the Town of Sweet Pickles, the animals get into and out of pickles because of their all too human personality traits.

Each of the books in the *Sweet Pickles* series is about a different pickle.

This book is about a rainy day and what everybody in town does about it.

Weekly Reader Books offers several exciting
card and activity programs. For information,
write to WEEKLY READER BOOKS, P.O. Box 16636,
Columbus, Ohio 43216.

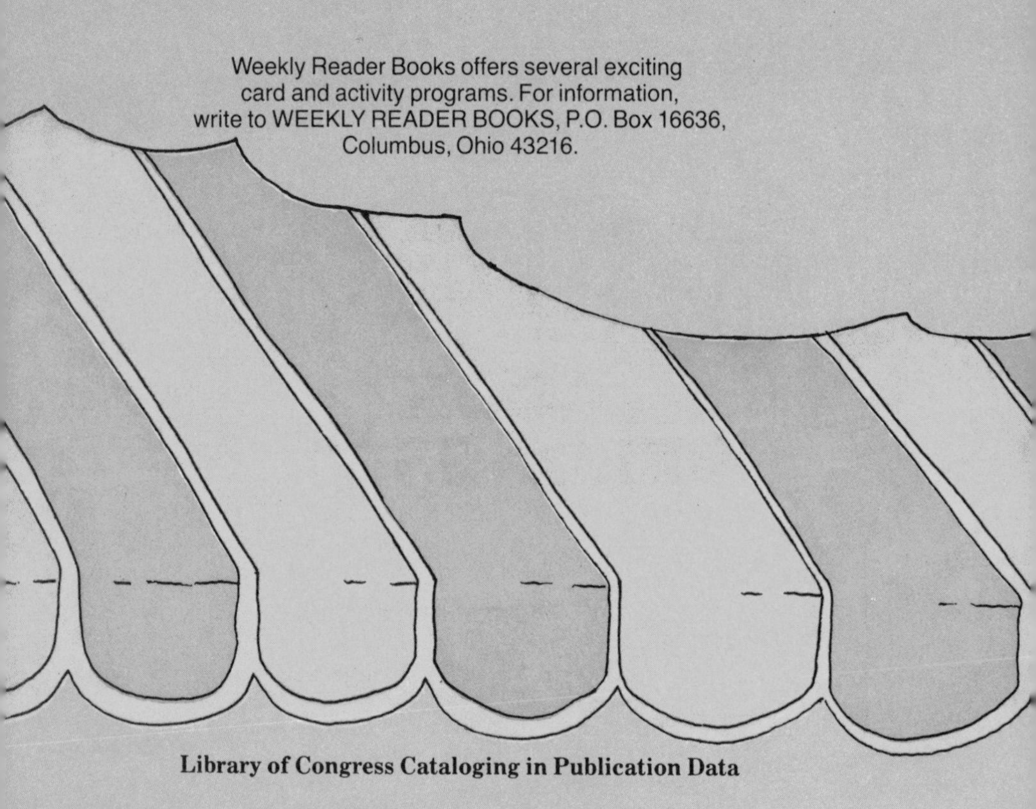

Library of Congress Cataloging in Publication Data

Reinach, Jacquelyn.
Rainy day parade.

(Sweet Pickles series)
SUMMARY: Zany Zebra shows the residents of the town of Sweet Pickles that a rainy day can be a wonderful day.
[1. Animals—Fiction. 2. Rain and rainfall—Fiction] I. Hefter, Richard. II. Title.
III. Series.
PZ7.R2747Rai [E] 80-19071
ISBN 0-937524-01-8

Published by Euphrosyne, Inc.

Printed in the United States of America

Weekly Reader Books' Edition

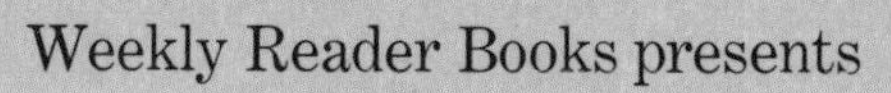

Weekly Reader Books presents

RAINY DAY PARADE

Written by Jacquelyn Reinach
Illustrated by Richard Hefter
Edited by Ruth Lerner Perle

It was a rainy and windy day. It was a gray and gloomy day. Everybody in the Town of Sweet Pickles was complaining about the weather.

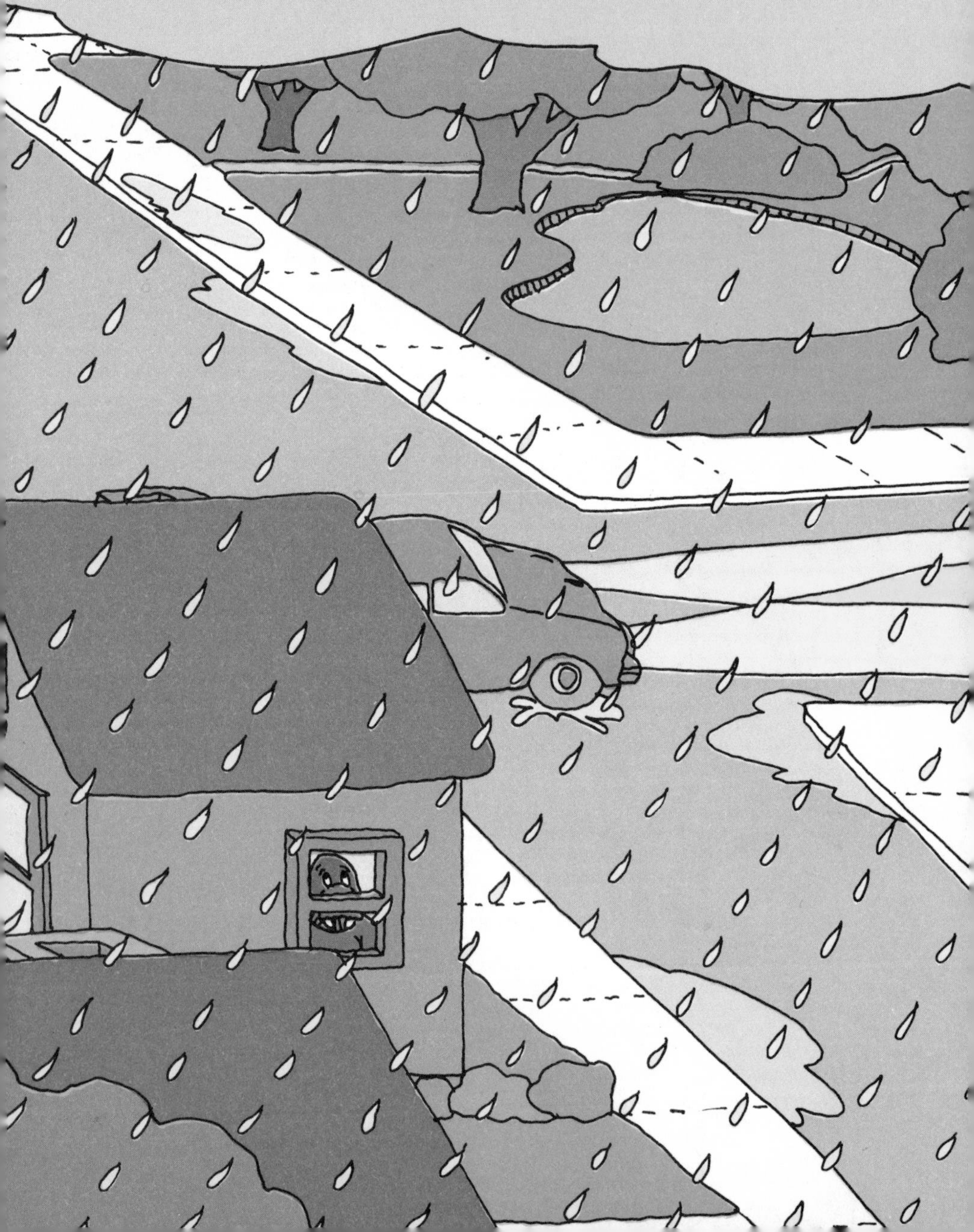

Accusing Alligator sat by the window in her ground floor apartment. The rain beat down.

"What a terrible day!" groaned Alligator. She turned on the weather report. "Rain continuing through tonight and tomorrow," it said.

"Stupid rain!" shouted Alligator. "It's all *your* fault! Now I can't even take a walk!"

Upstairs, Doubtful Dog and Imitating Iguana were also watching the rain.

"What a terrible day!" moaned Dog. "Look at all that rain. There's nothing to do!"

"Nothing to do!" said Iguana.

Down the street, Vain Vulture watched puddles grow in his front yard.

"Oh, no!" said Vulture. "I'm not going to work on a terrible day like this. I'll get my gorgeous feathers all wet!"

Up the block, Moody Moose listened to the rain on his roof.

"How awful!" he sniffed. "How sad! This weather is so bad I could cry!" And he did.

Way across town, Goof-Off Goose snuggled under her covers. "It's a terrible day!" she yawned. "I might as well stay in bed!" And she did.

Just then there was a loud clanging in the street.
Goose got up and opened the window. "What's going on?" she called.

It was Zany Zebra with a big drum and a small drum and a whistle and a flute and a huge umbrella with stripes.

"Listen, Zebra," shouted Goose, "all that clanging and banging and hooting and tooting is keeping me awake! And why are you out on such a terrible day anyway?"

"Why not?" giggled Zebra. "It's a perfectly *wonderful* day for having fun! Every day is! So, come on out and play, Goose. Put on your raincoat and boots and I'll share my umbrella with you."

"Not today," said Goose. "Maybe tomorrow."

"And later on," continued Zebra, "we'll go to my house and have hot chocolate and cookies!"

"*Cookies!*" smiled Goose. She threw on her raincoat, found a blue boot and a red boot and ran out to join Zebra.

Zebra and Goose splashed down Park Avenue. They stopped at the Tower Apartments and Zebra sang a wet and silly song. Goose laughed and laughed.

Everybody looked out.

"I don't see what there is to laugh about on such a terrible day!" called Dog.

"Anyone can laugh when it's nice out!" smiled Zebra. "Laughing when it's nasty takes some work. So come on out and help!"

"Well, all right," said Dog, putting on his boots. "I'm coming!"

"Me too!" said Iguana.

Then almost everyone in the building bundled up and went out to join Zebra. They splashed and sploshed and sang and danced all the way down the street.

They passed Vulture's house.

"Hmm," said Vulture. "This is a good chance to show off my new raincoat!" He ran out to join them.

Zebra led the parade all around town. Everybody ran out to join the fun.

It rained harder and harder.

Then Zebra blew his whistle. "It's raining much too hard now," he shouted. "Let's go back to my house for hot chocolate and cookies."

"No, no!" cried everyone. "We're having too much fun! Who wants to go inside on such a wonderful day?"

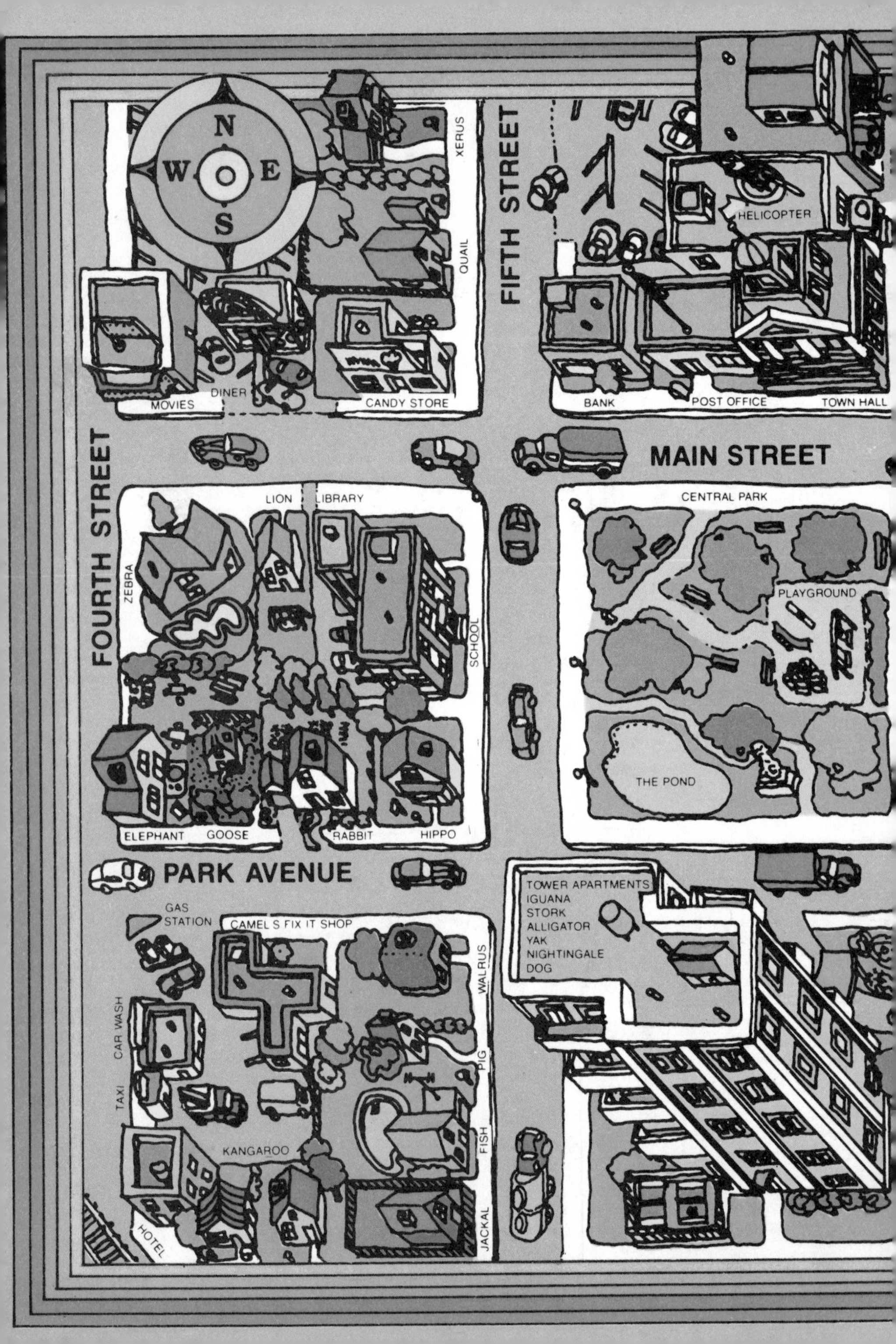
N
W
E
S
O
XERUS
QUAIL
FIFTH STREET
HELICOPTER
MOVIES
DINER
CANDY STORE
BANK
POST OFFICE
TOWN HALL
MAIN STREET
FOURTH STREET
LION
LIBRARY
CENTRAL PARK
ZEBRA
SCHOOL
PLAYGROUND
THE POND
ELEPHANT
GOOSE
RABBIT
HIPPO
PARK AVENUE
GAS STATION
CAMEL S FIX IT SHOP
TOWER APARTMENTS
IGUANA
STORK
ALLIGATOR
YAK
NIGHTINGALE
DOG
WALRUS
CAR WASH
PIG
TAXI
FISH
KANGAROO
HOTEL
JACKAL